The
Pen Pal Puzzle

In the front hallway, Nancy saw a big envelope on the floor near the mail slot. She ran to the window and looked out. Someone was just dashing around the corner.

Nancy picked up the envelope. A hand-drawn stamp of a weird monster was on the front. On the back was a return address:

> Vampire Pen Pal
> Big Graveyard
> London, England

Nancy opened the envelope. Inside was a drawing of a vampire. In a bubble over the vampire's head was a horrible message:

> "I suck the ink off letters
> and make them disappear."

The Nancy Drew Notebooks

Available from MINSTREL Books

#11

THE NANCY DREW NOTEBOOKS™

THE PEN PAL PUZZLE

CAROLYN KEENE

Illustrated by Anthony Accardo

A MINSTREL® BOOK

PUBLISHED BY POCKET BOOKS

New York   London   Toronto   Sydney   Tokyo   Singapore

A MINSTREL PAPERBACK *ORIGINAL*

 A Minstrel Book published by
POCKET BOOKS, a division of Simon & Schuster Inc.
1230 Avenue of the Americas, New York, NY 10020

Copyright © 1996 by Simon & Schuster Inc.
Produced by Mega-Books Inc.

ISBN: 0-671-53550-1

First Minstrel Books printing March 1996

10 9 8 7 6 5 4 3 2 1

NANCY DREW, A MINSTREL BOOK and colophon are registered trademarks of Simon & Schuster Inc.

THE NANCY DREW NOTEBOOKS is a trademark of Simon & Schuster Inc.

Cover art by Aleta Jenks

Printed in the U.S.A.

1

Poster Disaster

Give me that!" Brenda Carlton said. She grabbed a blue crayon from Nancy Drew's hand. Brenda took the crayon back to the table where she was sitting with Phoebe Archer.

Nancy's mouth turned down into a frown. She was used to Brenda acting selfish, but it still made her mad.

"Hasn't she ever heard of sharing?" Bess Marvin asked. She was one of Nancy's best friends.

"Yeah. She and Phoebe have plenty of crayons," George Fayne said. She nodded toward the other girls' table. It was next to the blackboard at the front of the classroom. "Brenda is just being mean."

George was Bess's cousin. She was also Nancy's other best friend. George was sitting at the same table with Nancy and Bess.

"She *is* mean." Nancy agreed. "But I'm not going to let her get me mad. I need to work on my pen pal poster."

Ms. Spencer's third-grade students were working on their pen pal project for their language arts class. Each student chose someone special to write a letter to. They learned how to address the envelope. They even learned how to look up a ZIP code to help make sure their letters got to the right place.

Now they were making posters for Parents' Night. The posters were all about the person to whom they had written letters.

George had written to a famous soccer player. He had sent her a big autographed photo of himself in his team uniform.

Bess's poster was all about her favorite book series. It included a letter she had received from the author.

Nancy's poster used letters she got from her pen pal, Pamela Morgan, who lived in England.

Pamela's parents were friends of Nancy's father. Pamela, her parents, and her brother, Derrick, had spent Thanksgiving with the Drews.

Pamela was the same age as Nancy—eight years old—but they had not gotten along at first. Nancy thought Pamela was stuck-up. But by the end of the visit, Pamela and Nancy were friends. Now they even wrote to each other.

Nancy loved to write letters. She also loved to get mail. A letter from Pamela was extra special. Nancy had saved every one of Pamela's letters.

Bess noticed the envelopes peeking out from underneath Nancy's poster board. "Those stamps are beautiful!" Bess said.

Nancy nodded. "I know. The stamps are the most important part of my poster."

Nancy felt a tug at the neck of her

sweater. Then something cold and slimy slithered down her back.

"Eek!" she yelled, and jumped up.

"Gotcha!" Mike Minelli said.

Quickly Nancy reached back and lifted the neck of her sweater. Something sticky and wet fell into her other hand.

"Ick! Is that a worm?" Bess asked. She looked as if she was going to be sick.

"No, it's a piece of spaghetti," George said, looking at the long white strand in Nancy's hand.

"Yuck!" Bess said. "Mike Minelli, you are gross."

"Mike!" Ms. Spencer's voice cut through the classroom. "Go back to your seat, please."

"Yeah, Mike. Go back to your seat," Bess echoed.

Mike went back to his seat. Nancy made a face. She tossed the spaghetti into the trash.

"How's your poster coming?" Nancy asked Bess.

Bess beamed. She was very proud of her poster. "I still can't believe a famous writer like Heather Talcott actually wrote me back."

"Was it scary to write to someone you didn't know?" Nancy asked.

"Was it ever! I must have used up a whole pad of lined paper. Finally I got it right. I told her my favorite Susie book was *Susie's Safari Adventure*. I wrote about how I got goose bumps when the Jeep broke down and Susie and her brother were trapped. I thought the lions would eat them for sure."

Bess shuddered, then continued cutting out pictures of wild animals from magazines to paste onto her poster.

"Susie couldn't get eaten by lions," George pointed out as she opened a jar of red paint. "She's the star of the books."

"She could *so* get eaten," Bess insisted. "Then the books would be all about her brother's adventures."

Nancy smiled. Bess and George almost

6

never agreed about anything. Even though they were cousins, Nancy's two best friends weren't at all alike. George—whose real name was Georgia—loved sports. She was the captain of her soccer team. Bess didn't like doing anything that got her clothes dirty.

The two cousins didn't look alike, either. Bess was blond, with sparkling blue eyes. She was a little shorter than Nancy. George had dark brown curly hair and brown eyes. She was taller than Nancy.

"My favorite Susie book was when she went scuba diving and found that old coin," Nancy said.

"Yeah! Then she figured out the coin came from a sunken ship," George added.

"I would never go scuba diving," Bess said. "I don't want to swim in the ocean. There are sharks!"

"May I have your attention, class?" At the sound of Ms. Spencer's voice, everyone looked up and stopped what they were doing.

Everyone except Jason Hutchings and Mike Minelli. Jason had two crayons hanging out of his mouth so they looked like fangs. Mike had two sticking out of his nose. They were clowning around as usual.

Ms. Spencer gave Mike and Jason a stern look. The boys put the crayons back on the table.

"Double gross," Bess whispered. "I don't want to use any of Mike's crayons. They were in his nose!"

"We'll be leaving for the post office field trip in ten minutes," Ms. Spencer said.

"But I've still got lots more monsters to draw," Mike complained. He had written to the United States Postal Service, asking them to issue a series of famous monster stamps. He'd gotten a letter back thanking him for the suggestion, but they weren't going to do the monster stamps. Mike decided he'd draw them himself.

"It's only Wednesday, Mike," Ms. Spencer said patiently. "You'll have time tomorrow and Friday to finish up your poster before Parents' Night. Now, everybody, hurry and clean up."

Nancy, Bess, and George started to clear their table. Ms. Spencer had set up a place at the back of the classroom to store the posters. Some of the students had already begun putting their posters away.

"Did you see Brenda's poster?" Bess asked. She made a face to show she didn't like it.

Nancy looked over to Brenda and Phoebe's table. Brenda was almost finished with her poster. It looked like the front page of a newspaper.

"I like Phoebe's poster better," Nancy said. "I think her dog is cute."

Phoebe had a picture of her cocker spaniel at the top of her poster. She had cut out dog pictures from magazines and pasted them in each corner. There was a bright blue border around the center, which was still blank.

Phoebe had written to the River Heights Dog Owners Society. She wanted to enter her dog in a dog show.

They had sent her a letter and an entry form. She was going to paste those in the center of her poster.

Nancy was about to carry her poster to the back of the room when Brenda brushed past Bess. Brenda's poster was shiny with wet paint.

"Watch out!" Bess cried. The paint almost touched her new shirt.

"Watch out yourself," Brenda said.

Nancy jumped back out of Brenda's way. She didn't want to get paint on her clothes either.

Nancy's hand hit something on the edge of the table. Then she heard a crash and a scream. When she turned, she saw Phoebe kneeling on the floor next to her poster. A jar of red paint had spilled all the way across the clean white center of Phoebe's poster!

2

The Missing Letters

"Oh, no! My poster!" Phoebe wailed. She looked as if she was about to cry.

"I'm sorry," Nancy said. "I didn't mean to."

"It's totally messed up," Brenda told Phoebe. She sounded almost pleased. "Nancy *ruined* your poster."

Phoebe sniffled.

"It was an accident!" Nancy protested. She felt awful. She could imagine how bad she would feel if her poster had gotten paint spilled on it.

Ms. Spencer came over and kneeled next to Phoebe's poster. She gave Phoebe some wet paper towels. They began to wipe up the paint with the wet paper towels.

"Wow! It looks like blood," Jason said. He leaned over to get a better view of Phoebe's poster.

"That gives me an idea," Mike Minelli said. He raced back to his own poster.

Ms. Spencer and Phoebe cleaned off most of the red paint. But there was still a big pink splotch across the center of Phoebe's poster.

"That's too bad about your poster, Phoebe," Brenda said. "I guess one clumsy person can really spoil everything." Brenda gave Nancy a nasty look.

"*You're* the clumsy one. You almost got paint on my shirt," Bess said.

"But I didn't, did I?" Brenda said in a snotty tone of voice. "Nancy is the one who got paint all over everything."

Nancy felt bad about knocking the paint over onto Phoebe's poster. All the mean things Brenda was saying made her feel even worse.

"I'm sorry, Phoebe," Nancy said again.

Phoebe didn't say anything. She just sniffled some more and glared at Nancy.

"Okay, girls," Ms. Spencer said. "It's almost time to go. The bus is waiting downstairs to take us to the post office for our field trip."

Nancy put the crayons she had been using back in their box. Then she put all the art supplies away near the back of the room. Bess tossed some magazine scraps in the wastepaper basket. George wiped off their table.

A few minutes later, everyone was lining up at the door to leave. They would stop at their cubbies in the hall to get their jackets on their way out.

"Hurry up, slowpoke!" Jason yelled to Mike. "You're the last one out."

"Okay, okay. I just had to add some blood to my vampire's fangs," Mike said. He rushed out to join the others.

"Oops, I forgot my backpack," Phoebe said. Phoebe came out a moment later with her backpack on one shoulder. She brushed past Nancy and joined Brenda at the cubbies.

13

Nancy bit her lip.

"She'll get over it," Bess said. She had already gotten her jacket from her cubby and was waiting for Nancy to get hers.

"I hope so," Nancy said. But she didn't think it would be any time soon.

"I love field trips," Nancy said as the bus pulled in next to the River Heights main post office.

"But a post office is boring," Bess said. She straightened her headband. "Why couldn't we go to a bakery or a chocolate factory instead? Now, *that* would be fun!"

"You liked getting a letter from a famous author," George reminded her cousin. *"That* wasn't boring."

Everyone got off the bus and lined up outside the door to the post office. A woman in a light blue uniform came outside and introduced herself. "Hi, my name is Mary Jo Donovan. I'm the postmaster here. First I'm going to give you a tour. Then I will answer any

14

questions you have about the mail and how it's delivered."

Ms. Donovan took the class inside the post office. She used a key to open a door marked Employees Only. Then she led them into a large room.

The postmaster introduced the class to several postal workers. They also wore light blue uniforms.

"Every morning we get bags and boxes of mail from all over the world," Ms. Donovan explained. "Over here is where we sort letters for delivery. Some of the letters go in the post office boxes over there. The others get sorted by route. Then each mail carrier sorts the letters for his or her route and bundles them with rubber bands."

The postmaster pointed to some machines up on a counter. "Here's where we weigh packages. This machine prints out a slip with the exact postage for each package."

"How much would it cost to send a person?" Jason asked. Several kids laughed at Jason's silly question.

"Well, that would depend on how much the person weighed, where you were sending him or her, and if the package was going first class," Ms. Donovan answered with a smile.

Nancy noticed Brenda and Phoebe whispering. Phoebe glanced up, and Nancy smiled at her. Instead of smiling back, Phoebe looked away.

"What's this?" George asked the postmaster, pointing to a large poster with pictures of lots of colorful stamps. *Philately* was written in big block letters across the top.

"It's pronounced fa-LAT-lee." Ms. Donovan said the word extra slowly. "Does anyone know what that means?" she asked.

Andrew Leoni raised his hand, and Ms. Donovan nodded at him.

"It means stamp collecting," Andrew said.

"Very good," Ms. Donovan said. "Stamp collecting is a popular hobby. In fact, when I was your age, I collected stamps. That's one reason I wanted to work in a post office."

After the tour of the post office, Ms. Donovan said good-bye. Ms. Spencer led the class back to the bus. Soon they were back at Carl Sandburg Elementary School.

"It's almost time to go home," Ms. Spencer said as the bus door opened. "Hurry and get what you need from the classroom and your cubbies."

Nancy was the first one back inside the classroom.

"Are we racing?" Bess asked, trying to catch her breath.

"No," Nancy answered. "I remembered I left the letters from Pamela in my desk. I want to take them home with me."

Nancy reached inside her desk, but she didn't feel anything. I know I left them here, Nancy said to herself. She bent down to look.

The letters were gone!

3

Nancy Is on the Case

They're not here!" Nancy looked inside her desk a second time. "My letters are gone!"

"Maybe they fell out and got thrown away when we were cleaning up," George suggested.

Nancy told Ms. Spencer about the missing letters. Ms. Spencer asked the class to help Nancy look for them.

George looked through the wastepaper baskets. Bess looked under all the desks. Nancy checked the boxes that held the art supplies they had been using.

Nancy noticed that Brenda and Phoebe weren't helping. Instead they were whispering and giggling.

I wonder if they took my letters, Nancy thought. She remembered that Phoebe had run back inside the classroom after everyone else had gone to the cubbies.

Could Phoebe have taken them to get even with her for spilling paint on her poster? Would Phoebe be that mean?

The bell rang, and Ms. Spencer dismissed the class.

"Too bad about your letters," Brenda said as she passed Nancy on her way out. But Brenda didn't sound sorry.

"Yeah, too bad," Phoebe echoed. She followed Brenda out, clutching her poster. She was taking it home to try to fix it.

A few minutes later, Nancy and Bess and George were the only students left in the classroom. They were still looking for the letters.

"It's time to go home, girls," Ms. Spencer said.

"But we haven't found Nancy's letters," Bess said.

"We'll look some more tomorrow,"

Ms. Spencer said. She put her hand on Nancy's shoulder. "I'm sure they'll turn up," she said.

But Nancy wasn't so sure.

Nancy spotted the familiar car as soon as she stepped out of the school building. Hannah Gruen was waiting to take Nancy to the mall. They were going to buy new sneakers for Nancy.

Hannah was the Drew family's housekeeper. She had lived with the Drews and taken care of Nancy ever since Nancy's mother died.

"How was your day?" Hannah asked as Nancy fastened her seat belt.

"Not so good," Nancy answered. She told Hannah about the missing letters.

"Sounds like a mystery to me," Hannah said. Hannah knew that Nancy liked to solve mysteries.

Was it a mystery if you knew who did it? Nancy wondered.

Nancy was pretty sure that Phoebe had taken her letters. But she knew it would be wrong to accuse her classmate until she had proof. So she didn't say anything more about it to Hannah.

As soon as she got home, Nancy rushed to her room. Hannah was right. This was a mystery, and Nancy had to solve it quickly. Parents' Night was only two days away.

Nancy opened her desk drawer and took out a small notebook with a shiny blue cover. Nancy's father had given her the blue notebook. She always used it when she had a mystery to solve. She wrote about suspects and clues in it.

Nancy flipped to the first clean page. At the top she wrote "Missing Letters." She thought for a moment, then wrote "Lost or Stolen?"

Nancy didn't think they were lost. George had checked all the wastepaper baskets, and the letters weren't anywhere in the classroom. Someone had to have taken them. She crossed out "Lost."

On the next line she wrote "Suspects."

The first suspect was obvious. Nancy wrote "Phoebe" on the next line. Phoebe was angry at Nancy for spilling the red paint on her poster. And she did run back into the classroom right before the field trip. She could have taken the letters from Nancy's desk then.

What about Brenda? Nancy didn't like Brenda. She went out of her way to be mean to Nancy. It would be just like Brenda to take the letters to cause trouble.

Nancy wrote "Brenda" on the next line.

"Nancy!" Hannah called from the kitchen. "Don't forget to do your homework."

How did Hannah know she wasn't doing her homework? Nancy groaned.

She put her blue notebook back in her desk drawer. Then she took her math workbook out of her backpack.

Nancy was good at math. She did the ten multiplication problems quickly. Then she checked her work.

As she was putting her workbook

back in her backpack, she heard something downstairs. It sounded as if it came from near the front door.

It was too early for her father to be home. Nancy was curious. What caused that sound? She ran downstairs to see.

When Nancy got to the front hallway, she saw a big envelope on the floor near the mail slot. She heard footsteps outside. Nancy ran to the window and looked out. Someone was just dashing around the corner.

Someone wearing a black-and-yellow jacket.

It took Nancy a moment to remember where she had seen that jacket before. Someone in her class had been wearing a jacket just like it on the field trip to the post office.

Nancy thought and thought. She pictured the jacket in her mind. Then she tried to picture the person's face.

Finally it came to her, and she said the name out loud.

"Mike Minelli!"

4

A Monster Clue

Nancy picked up the envelope. A hand-drawn stamp of a weird monster was on the front. On the back was a return address:

Vampire Pen Pal
Big Graveyard
London, England

Nancy opened the envelope. Inside was a drawing of a vampire. In a bubble over the vampire's head were the words "I suck the ink off letters and make them disappear."

"Disappear"? Could Mike have made the letters from Pamela disappear? Was

Mike playing one of his dumb jokes? He was always playing tricks on Nancy and her friends.

This was definitely an important clue. Nancy had to write about it in her notebook.

Nancy ran upstairs to her room and took out her blue notebook again. Under "Suspects" she added a new name, "Mike Minelli."

Now she had three suspects: Phoebe, Brenda, and Mike.

She wrote a new heading: "Clues."

Mike was the last one out of the classroom. He could have taken the letters then. And Phoebe ran back inside to get her backpack. She could have taken them, too. Nancy wrote all that down in her notebook.

Nancy remembered Phoebe and Brenda whispering at the post office. Maybe Phoebe was telling Brenda that she had the letters.

This case was getting complicated. And Nancy had only two days to solve it.

"Pudding Pie? I'm home," Nancy heard her father calling up the stairs. Pudding Pie was one of his favorite nicknames for her. He had called her that ever since she was four years old. That's when Nancy had tried to eat a huge piece of chocolate pudding pie with her hands. She had gotten chocolate all over her face! It was even in her hair. Her father had taken a picture of her looking like that. It was in one of their photo albums.

Maybe Dad can help me solve this case, Nancy thought as she ran downstairs.

Carson Drew was a lawyer. He knew all about mysteries and crimes. He was always solving problems for other people. Nancy hoped he could help her solve this mystery.

Over dinner she told her father all about the missing letters and her three suspects.

"It sounds like a tough case," he said. "But you're a good detective. And you've always been good at finding things."

Nancy knew her father was right. She *was* good at finding things. But she didn't have any idea where to look this time.

"Detectives usually interview their suspects. Why don't you call Mike after dinner and ask him about your letters?" Mr. Drew suggested.

After dinner, Nancy called Mike Minelli. Mrs. Minelli answered the phone.

"This is Nancy Drew," Nancy said politely. "May I please speak with Mike?"

"Of course, Nancy," Mrs. Minelli said. Nancy heard Mrs. Minelli yell, "Mike, phone. It's Nancy Drew."

A few seconds later, Mike picked up the phone. "Hello?" Mike said. His voice sounded hoarse.

"Did you slip a letter through the mail slot at my house this afternoon?" Nancy asked. She was pretty sure it was him because she had recognized his jacket.

29

"Maybe," Mike answered. He sneezed loudly into the phone.

"Did you take my pen pal letters from my desk today?" Nancy continued.

"Why would I want *your* pen pal letters," Mike said. "I have my own pen pal—a monster pen pal."

"But you were the last person to leave the classroom. You could have taken them then," Nancy persisted.

"Maybe one of my monsters ate your letters while we were at the post office," Mike suggested.

Mike was so weird!

"If you did take them, will you give them back before Parents' Night?" Nancy asked.

"If I did take them, I might." Mike sneezed again. Nancy heard Mrs. Minelli's voice in the background. "I have to go," Mike said.

"Okay," Nancy said. "Good-bye." Nancy hung up the phone and went upstairs to get ready for bed. She changed into her pajamas. Then she washed her face and brushed her teeth.

When she was in bed, her father came in to read to her. But Nancy couldn't concentrate on the story. She kept thinking about her missing letters and her poster for Parents' Night.

She was pretty sure Mike had left the monster pen pal letter for her. Maybe he had taken Pamela's letters. Maybe . . .

But Nancy never finished that thought. She was already fast asleep.

The sun woke Nancy the next morning. It was so bright. Nancy felt happy. She washed up and put on her favorite jeans and a blue sweater. Then she took her new sneakers out of their box and slipped them on. They were the same shade of blue as her sweater.

It wasn't until she went downstairs for breakfast that she remembered she had to find her missing letters by the next afternoon.

"Good morning, Nancy," Hannah said. She placed a stack of pancakes down on the table. The butter and syrup were already there next to a glass of milk and a glass of orange juice.

"Thanks, Hannah," Nancy said as she sat down. She sipped her juice. Even though pancakes was one of her favorite breakfasts, she didn't have much of an appetite. She was worried about her poster.

"Will you drive me to school today, Hannah?" Nancy asked. "I want to get there early to look for my letters."

"Okay, dear. You finish eating, and I'll go find my car keys."

Hannah dropped Nancy at school fifteen minutes early. Nancy left her jacket in her cubby and rushed into her classroom. Ms. Spencer was already there.

"Did you find my letters?" Nancy asked, breathless.

"No, Nancy. But I have an idea for your poster. You can write a report about what was in Pamela's letters and describe what the stamps looked like.

Then you can put the report on your poster."

"But that won't look as good," Nancy said. "I need the real stamps or my poster will be ugly."

"I'm sorry, Nancy," Ms. Spencer said. "That was the only idea I came up with."

By now several other students had come in.

Nancy took her poster from the back of the room. Sadly, she started to write her report. But her heart wasn't in it. She took out her blue notebook. She had brought it with her to school so she could keep trying to solve the mystery.

Nancy felt someone watching her and looked up. George and Bess were standing next to her chair. Nancy hadn't noticed them come in.

"Uh-oh," George said, putting her poster down on the table. George knew that when Nancy took out her special notebook, there was a mystery to solve. "I guess this means Detective Drew is on the case of the missing letters."

"So who are your suspects?" Bess asked.

"I'll bet Phoebe is a suspect," George whispered as Phoebe walked into the classroom.

"Hi, Phoebe," Nancy said.

Phoebe ignored Nancy.

Nancy noticed that Phoebe wasn't carrying her poster. She must have left it at home.

"She's definitely still mad at you," Bess said. "That's a clue."

"Yes," Nancy agreed. "She *is* a suspect. But I have other suspects, too." She told them about Brenda. She also told them about Mike Minelli's letter.

"Mike's not here today," Bess said happily. "Maybe we can have at least one day of peace."

"I called Mike last night, and he was sneezing. Maybe he has a cold and stayed home," Nancy said.

"Or maybe he feels guilty because he took your letters," George said.

"Not Mike. Mike never feels guilty about *anything*," Bess said.

After working on their posters for an hour, the class reviewed their math homework.

Finally it was time for lunch. Nancy, Bess, and George sat together at their usual table.

Nancy ate her tuna sandwich without tasting it. She was thinking about her missing letters.

"Why don't you just make Phoebe give you back your letters?" Bess asked.

"I don't have any proof that she took them." Nancy sighed unhappily.

"You could ask her," George suggested.

"All right, I will." Nancy got up and walked over to where Phoebe and Brenda were sitting. They were talking and laughing. When they saw her, they stopped and stared at her.

"What do *you* want?' Brenda asked. Nancy wished Brenda weren't there.

"Phoebe," Nancy said, ignoring Brenda, "my pen pal letters are missing."

"Are you accusing Phoebe of *steal-*

ing?" Brenda interrupted in a loud voice. Several students turned to look at them.

Nancy could feel her face get hot. "I thought you might have seen them."

"I didn't take your letters!" Phoebe shouted. "Now leave us alone!"

Nancy walked back to her table. She was no closer to finding her letters than before.

5

Returned Letters

After lunch Nancy's class studied spelling and science. Nancy tried to concentrate on her work, but her mind kept drifting back to her missing letters.

Nancy glanced over at Phoebe. Phoebe was still Nancy's main suspect. But Nancy still had no proof. She needed a clue. Nancy decided she'd watch Phoebe extra carefully at school.

"Ms. Spencer." Phoebe waved her hand in the air to get the teacher's attention.

"Yes, Phoebe?" Ms. Spencer said.

"May I go to the bathroom?"

Ms. Spencer nodded, and Phoebe

went up to the front of the class to get the bathroom pass.

"Me, too," Brenda said, waving her hand in the air. "I have to go, too."

"Okay, Brenda," Ms. Spencer said.

Nancy watched Brenda and Phoebe rush out the door. They almost collided with Andrew Leoni.

"Why don't you watch where you're going!" Brenda said loudly.

"Why don't you?" Andrew said.

Nancy noticed Andrew was rubbing his arm where Brenda had bumped into him.

Phoebe must have noticed, too. "Did you hurt your arm?" she asked him

"Nah." Andrew shook his head. "I just got a shot at the doctor's. It's a little sore."

"Phoebe, come on," Brenda ordered. "We don't have all day."

Nancy wondered why Phoebe was hanging around with Brenda. Brenda was always bossing her around.

After Brenda and Phoebe returned, Ms. Spencer announced it was time for reading. "I want everyone to pair up and read to each other. You may choose any book you like," she said.

Nancy loved reading. She was paired with Bess. George was paired with Emily Reeves.

"Can we read from your fairy tale book?" Bess asked. "The one you got from the library?"

"Sure," Nancy said. "I left it in my cubby on the bottom shelf."

Bess asked permission to go to the cubbies. A moment later she was back with the book.

Nancy liked fairy tales. She and Bess took turns reading to each other. The reading period flew by. When the final bell rang, Nancy and Bess walked out together. They stopped at Nancy's cubby first. Bess put Nancy's book back where she found it. Then she went to her own cubby to get her jacket.

"Want to go with me to the Bell on the way home?" Bess asked. The Bell was short for the School Bell, a small store near the school.

"Okay. Is George coming with us?" Nancy asked.

"No. She has to work on her book report," Bess said.

Nancy took her jacket off the hook. She noticed something on the top shelf of her cubby: several folded pieces of paper.

What are these? she wondered. They weren't here when I got back from lunch.

She reached for them and gasped.

Pamela's letters!

Bess threw her arms around Nancy and hugged her. "That's great. You have your letters back. Now your poster will be perfect!"

Nancy flipped through the letters. All four of them were there. "But the envelopes with the stamps on them are still missing," Nancy said. She rummaged through her cubby. "I need the stamps for my poster, too."

Together, Bess and Nancy removed everything from Nancy's cubby. They shook out every book and checked the

pockets of her jacket. But the envelopes weren't there.

Finally they realized they had to leave. They put on their jackets and walked out of the school building. A few minutes later, they were at the Bell.

"At least now you know for sure someone took them," Bess said as she picked out a pink Day-Glo marker.

"Yes, but why would the thief return only the letters?" Nancy wondered out loud.

"Maybe Phoebe still wants to get even with you for ruining her poster. She knows you need the stamps, so she's keeping them."

"Maybe," Nancy said. "But that sounds more like something Brenda would do." She paused to think. "Maybe Phoebe wanted to give everything back," Nancy said, "but Brenda talked her into keeping the stamps. Maybe that's why Brenda asked to go to the bathroom when Phoebe did. They could have put the letters back in my cubby then."

43

"Maybe," Bess agreed. "Maybe they'll return the envelopes tomorrow."

"Maybe," Nancy said. But she didn't think so.

Bess paid for her marker. Nancy flipped through a comic book, but she decided not to buy it.

Hannah was in the kitchen when Nancy got home. Hannah sliced an apple, and Nancy ate it with peanut butter. After her snack, Nancy took out her blue notebook.

Who could have put the letters back in my cubby? she asked herself. The letters weren't there when she'd hung up her jacket after lunch. Who had left the classroom that afternoon?

Phoebe and Brenda were still suspects. They had left the classroom together to go to the bathroom. They could have put the letters back then.

Mike Minelli was out sick all day, so he couldn't have put the letters back. That meant he didn't take them in the first place. Nancy drew a line through

Mike's name. He was no longer a suspect.

Nancy remembered that Andrew Leoni had come back from his doctor's appointment just when Phoebe and Brenda were leaving the classroom. She wrote his name under suspects. But why would he have taken her letters in the first place?

Nancy still thought Phoebe was the best suspect.

"Hannah, may I bike over to Phoebe Archer's house?" Nancy asked.

"Okay, but don't forget to walk your bike when you cross the street," Hannah instructed. "And don't stay too long. Your father's taking you out for pizza tonight."

"Yum!" Pizza was one of Nancy's favorite foods.

Nancy didn't tell Hannah the real reason she wanted to go to Phoebe's house. She was going to look for clues. Maybe Phoebe had left the envelopes out somewhere and Nancy could see them.

Nancy biked over to the Archers'

house. When she got there, she noticed the lights were on in the kitchen. Being extra quiet, Nancy got off her bike and crept over to the kitchen window. Maybe Phoebe was in there. Maybe she had the envelopes with her. Nancy hoped so.

Nancy sneaked over to the kitchen window, but it was too high for her to see in. She looked around for something to stand on. There was an old orange crate next to the side of the house by the recycling bin. Nancy moved the crate under the window and climbed up onto it.

But before Nancy got a good look through the window, there was a loud *crack!*

The slats of the crate snapped in two. With a loud clatter, Nancy tumbled to the ground!

6

Stamp Collector
Suspect

What was that?" Nancy recognized Phoebe's voice. A moment later Phoebe leaned out the window. She looked down right at Nancy. "Are you all right?" Phoebe asked.

Nancy got up quickly and brushed herself off. "I'm fine." She tried to think of some excuse for why she was peeking into Phoebe's kitchen window.

"What happened? Did you trip over that crate?" Phoebe asked.

Nancy nodded. She was relieved she didn't have to lie about what she was doing.

"I'm really glad you're here," Phoebe continued. "I was going to call you to tell you about my poster." Phoebe didn't sound angry anymore. "Come in, I'll show you."

Nancy walked around to the back door and went inside. Phoebe's poster was on the kitchen table. Phoebe had painted the entire area inside the blue border a bright pink. Now the pink splotch hardly showed at all.

"Wow!" Nancy said. "It looks great."

"I think so, too. If you hadn't spilled paint on it, I wouldn't have painted it pink. The entry form will show up much better against the pink background."

"I'm glad," Nancy said. But inside she was feeling jealous. Phoebe's poster was better than ever. Nancy's own poster would look even more boring in comparison—unless she found her stamps.

"I'm sorry about how I acted yesterday," Phoebe said. "I know it was an accident. I was mad, and I took it out on you."

"That's okay," Nancy said. "I know how you felt."

"That's right," Phoebe said. "I almost forgot. You lost your letters." Phoebe thought for a moment. "My mom has a friend in France who writes to her a lot. I could get those envelopes for you."

"Thanks, but the envelopes really have to be from England," Nancy said.

The front door slammed, and Phoebe's big brother came into the kitchen. "Hey," he said as he opened the refrigerator and rummaged around inside.

"Hi, Tim," Nancy said. Tim was in the sixth grade. She sometimes saw him in the hall at school.

Tim fixed himself a huge sandwich. He used three slices of bread and most of a package of sliced ham.

"Shee ya," he said with his mouth full on his way out.

Nancy said good-bye to Phoebe and biked home. She no longer thought that

Phoebe had taken her stamps. Nancy was running out of suspects. Even worse, she was running out of time.

When she got home, she saw George walking away from her front door. George had her in-line skates slung over her shoulder.

"George! Wait up!" Nancy yelled. She pedaled faster to catch up.

"Hi," George said. "Do you want to go skating?"

"Sure!" Nancy loved to skate. She ran into the house for her skates.

She and George practiced skating backward. They were still skating half an hour later when Mr. Drew's car pulled into the driveway.

"Hi, Pudding Pie." He gave Nancy a big hug. "Are you ready for pizza?"

"I'm always ready for pizza," Nancy said.

"Would you like to come with us, George?" Mr. Drew asked.

"I can't," George said. "Mom's expecting me home for dinner"—she looked at her watch—"oops, right now! I'd better hurry!"

"Bye!" Nancy and her father called as George skated toward her house.

Later, at the pizzeria, Nancy told her father about finding the letters in her cubby. "But the envelopes with the stamps on them are still missing," she said sadly. "My poster won't be very good without them."

Nancy finished her slice of pizza. She wiped her mouth and hands on a paper napkin.

"Did you bring your detective's notebook?" her father asked.

Nancy nodded. She took her notebook out of her jacket pocket. She had been carrying it with her all the time in case she had an idea or found a clue.

"So who are your suspects?" her father asked.

Nancy read her list of suspects. "Phoebe was my first suspect. But I don't think she did it anymore.

"Brenda was my second suspect. I thought she and Phoebe were ganging up on me. She and Phoebe were out of the classroom right before I found the letters in my cubby. But Brenda couldn't have put the letters there without Phoebe seeing her.

"Then there's Mike Minelli. But he wasn't in school today so he couldn't have returned the letters."

"No more suspects?" Mr. Drew asked.

Nancy looked at the last name on her list: Andrew Leoni.

"There is one more suspect," Nancy began. "Andrew Leoni. He came back from a doctor's appointment right before I found the letters in my cubby. He could have put them there. But he didn't have a reason to take them in the first place."

"No motive. Hmm." Mr. Drew rubbed the bridge of his nose. He was thinking hard. "Maybe he has a motive you haven't thought of," Mr. Drew suggested. "Sometimes the best way to solve a problem is to think about something totally different. Let's get your mind off the case for a while. Tell me about your field trip yesterday."

Nancy told her father all about the trip to the post office. "The postmaster said she collected stamps," Nancy continued. "That's why she wanted to work in a post office. We even saw a big poster about stamp collecting— That's it!" Nancy almost spilled her drink she was so excited. "Andrew knew the word for stamp collecting that was on the poster. Maybe *he* collects stamps. That would give him the perfect motive."

"Good detective work, Nancy." Her father smiled proudly at her. "I think you've earned some dessert. How about an ice cream cone?"

Nancy and her father stopped at the ice cream parlor on their way home. Nancy got a double dip cone with chocolate and strawberry ice cream. It took a long time to eat it. By the time they got home, it was almost Nancy's bedtime.

Nancy brushed her teeth and

changed into her nightgown. When her father came in to kiss her good night, Nancy asked, "Do you think Andrew will give me back my stamps?"

Mr. Drew nodded. "I think so. You can be pretty convincing," he said with a smile.

Nancy hoped her father was right. She closed her eyes and tried to fall asleep quickly. She was in a hurry for tomorrow to come, so she could talk Andrew into giving her back the stamps.

7

Where Are the Stamps?

Nancy got to school early Friday morning. She wanted to talk to Andrew before class started. But Andrew slipped into his seat just before the first bell. She'd have to wait.

It took forever until it was time for morning recess. Nancy was the first one out of her seat. But Andrew sat closer to the door. He was already at his cubby when Nancy caught up to him.

"Andrew! Wait!" Nancy called to him.

"Hi, Nancy," Andrew said.

"Andrew, did you take my letters?" Nancy blurted out.

Andrew's face turned red. He looked

down at his sneakers. Then he nodded slowly.

"So you'll give them back now?" she asked hopefully. There was still time to put them on her poster. Parents' Night wasn't going to be a disaster after all.

"I already put your letters back in your cubby yesterday," Andrew said, surprised. "Didn't you find them?"

"Only the letters. Not the envelopes," Nancy said. "I need the envelopes for the stamps for my poster."

"I put the stamps in your cubby, too. Underneath your book." Andrew went over to Nancy's cubby. "They're right here. See?" He lifted up the book of fairy tales.

The stamps weren't there.

"But I put them there! Honest!" Andrew was really upset. Nancy felt sorry for him. But she felt even sorrier for herself. She still didn't have the envelopes with the stamps. And Parents' Night was only hours away!

Andrew kept looking under the book of fairy tales as if he expected the stamps to magically appear. "They *have* to be here," he said.

"You took my letters because you collect stamps, right?" Nancy asked.

"Yeah," Andrew admitted. "Those stamps were exactly what I needed for my collection. While you were putting the art supplies away, before the field trip, I sneaked them out of your desk. That night I soaked the stamps off the envelopes. But then I felt really guilty. I never stole anything before. And I knew you needed the stamps for your poster."

"So then what did you do?" Nancy asked.

"The envelopes were all mushy from being in the warm water. The ink had run all over, so I threw them away."

Nancy thought about how much she liked seeing her name printed on the front of those envelopes. She swallowed hard.

"Then I pressed the stamps under some heavy books so they would dry flat," Andrew continued. "Yesterday I took the letters and stamps with me to school. I put them in your cubby when I came back from my doctor's appointment. I put the stamps under your book of fairy tales so they wouldn't get wrinkled or lost."

But they got lost anyway, Nancy thought sadly. Now it looked as if they were gone forever.

"I can't believe Andrew stole your letters," Bess said.

Nancy was eating lunch with Bess and George. She had just finished describing what had happened.

"Are you going to tell Ms. Spencer?" George asked.

Nancy thought about that. It wasn't right to steal, but Andrew had tried to return everything. "No," Nancy said. "I won't tell on him. He said he was sorry. Besides, telling won't get my stamps back."

"So what *are* you going to do?" George asked. "Parents' Night is tonight."

"I know," Nancy said. "Bess, are you

sure you didn't see the stamps when you borrowed my book?"

"I'm really, really double sure," Bess said. "I just pulled the book out and ran back to class."

"Maybe the stamps fell on the floor when Bess pulled out the book," George said.

Nancy was afraid George was right. Anyone could have picked up the stamps or thrown them away. How would she ever find them now?

School was almost over. Ms. Spencer's class spent last period finishing their posters and cleaning up the classroom for Parents' Night.

Now Ms. Spencer was helping the students tack their posters to the bulletin boards. Nancy had written the report as Ms. Spencer had suggested. But without the stamps, her poster didn't look very good, especially next to the others.

Nancy still wasn't ready to give up. Maybe the school custodian had found them when he swept up the day before.

It was a slim chance, but it was Nancy's last hope.

"Ms. Spencer? May I go ask Mr. Ingstrom if he saw my stamps?"

"Yes, you may," Ms. Spencer said. "But hurry."

Nancy wanted to run to Mr. Ingstrom's office. But she knew running in the halls was not allowed. So she walked very, very fast.

The door to Mr. Ingstrom's office was open. Nancy was happy to see that he was inside.

"Mr. Ingstrom?" she said as she knocked on the open door. "My name is Nancy Drew. I'm in Ms. Spencer's third-grade class. I lost some special stamps yesterday. They fell out of my cubby. Did you see them when you were cleaning up?"

"Hmm." Mr. Ingstrom took off his glasses and rubbed his eyes. "Now that you mention it, I think I did see them. I swept some stamps into my dust pile. Then a girl tapped me on the shoulder and asked if she could have them. I

didn't realize what they were till she picked them out and showed them to me. I said sure, she could have them. And that's the last I saw of her or the stamps."

"Do you know the name of the girl?" Nancy asked hopefully.

"No, but she was older than you— fifth or sixth grade, I'd guess." Mr. Ingstrom put his glasses back on his nose. "If you children took better care of your things, you wouldn't always—"

Nancy didn't have time to listen to his lecture. She had to find that girl, whoever she was. But how?

"Thanks, Mr. Ingstrom," Nancy said as she turned and left his office. She hurried down the hall.

Maybe the girl was a stamp collector like Andrew Leoni. Nancy was walking past the school library when she got an idea.

The librarian wasn't at her desk, but Nancy knew how to use the card catalog. She looked up stamp collecting.

There was only one book on the subject. She rushed to the shelves.

The book was there! Now all she had to do was look at the sign-out card. Everyone had to write their name and class number on the card when they took out a book. Maybe the girl who had her stamps had taken out this book.

Nancy opened the book. Was she about to solve the mystery?

8

Parents' Night

Nancy ran her finger down the list of names and class numbers on the card. There weren't many.

She saw Andrew's name and class number. Mr. Ingstrom had said a girl had taken the stamps. There were only two girls' names on the card. One was in a second-grade class. But Mr. Ingstrom had said the girl was older than Nancy, so it couldn't have been her. The other girl—Maya Chavez—was a sixth-grader!

Nancy crossed her fingers, hoping that Maya was the one who had her stamps. If she could find Maya, she might get her stamps back in time for Parents' Night.

Nancy put the library book on the cart to be reshelved. She left the library just as the bell rang.

Nancy dashed down the hall. All the classes were letting out for the day. If she hurried, she might catch Maya. But how would she recognize her?

"Nancy!" George called as she walked out of Ms. Spencer's class. "What's up?"

"I think I know who has my stamps," Nancy said, breathless. "It's a sixth-grader named Maya Chavez. I've got to try to find her. Tell Ms. Spencer I'll be right back."

"Okay," George said as Nancy sped off.

Nancy rounded the corner just as two classes of sixth-graders poured into the hallway.

Nancy looked around. There were so many sixth-grade girls. Which one was Maya?

Maybe I should just shout out her name, Nancy thought.

Then Nancy spotted Phoebe's brother, Tim. He was in the sixth grade. Maybe he knew Maya.

"Tim!" Nancy called. "Tim Archer!"

Tim turned around. "Oh, hi, Nancy," he said.

"Tim, do you know Maya Chavez?" Nancy asked in a rush. "I *have* to find her. It's really, really important."

"Sure," Tim said. "No problem. She's right over there. With the red sweater."

"Thanks!" Nancy called as she raced toward the girl Tim had pointed out.

Please, please, please, Nancy said to herself as she ran, please have my stamps!

Nancy almost collided with the tall girl in the red sweater. "Are you Maya Chavez?" she asked, breathing hard.

"Yes," Maya said. "Who are you?"

"My name is Nancy Drew. I lost some stamps yesterday in the hallway. They were from England. Did you find them?"

"Yes, I did," Maya said, amazed. "How did you know?"

"I don't have time to explain right now. But I would really appreciate it if I could have them back. Do you have them with you?"

"They're right here." Maya carefully opened her history book. The stamps were inside. She handed them to Nancy. "Wow! I can't believe you figured out I had them. You must be a great detective."

"Maybe someday I will be. Thanks," Nancy said. She took the stamps and rushed back to her own classroom. George and Bess were waiting there for her. So was Ms. Spencer and Andrew Leoni.

"You found them!" Bess said. She gave Nancy a big hug.

Nancy attached her stamps to her poster with little loops of tape.

When she was done, her poster looked great!

*　　*　　*

"So where's your poster, Pudding Pie?" Nancy's father teased her. Nancy's was right in front of him.

"Here, Daddy," Nancy said. She pointed proudly at her poster.

"It's beautiful," Mr. Drew said. "You did a great job. With the poster *and* with the case."

After everyone had looked at all the posters, they went to the refreshments table. There was coffee for the adults and juice for the students. There were also cookies and brownies.

"Time to go, Pudding Pie," Mr. Drew said as Nancy finished her cup of juice.

"Okay, Dad. In a minute. There's something I have to do first." Nancy walked over to where her poster was displayed. She carefully removed the stamps and took off the loops of tape. Then she found Andrew.

"Here." Nancy handed him the stamps.

"You're *giving* them to me?" Andrew

said, surprised. "Even after I took them and almost ruined your poster?"

Nancy nodded. "You should have asked me at the very beginning," she said. "I would have told you that you could have them after Parents' Night. You just had to ask."

"Thanks, Nancy," Andrew said. He held the stamps carefully, as if they were the most valuable stamps in the world. "Thanks a lot!"

That night before she went to bed, Nancy took out her blue notebook. She turned to a clean page and wrote:

I solved the mystery of the missing pen pal letters. It was really a double mystery—who took the letters and what happened to the stamps.

Maya was really nice to give me back my stamps, even after she found them fair and square. She knew they were important to me.

71

And Andrew was so happy to get the stamps after Parents' Night. Sometimes giving something away is even better than getting something in the first place.

Case closed.

Join eight-year old Nancy
and her best friends as they
collect clues and solve mysteries in

THE NANCY DREW NOTEBOOKS™

by **Carolyn Keene**
Illustrated by Anthony Accardo

A MINSTREL® BOOK

Published by Pocket Books

1045-05

FULL HOUSE™
Michelle

#1: THE GREAT PET PROJECT

#2: THE SUPER-DUPER SLEEPOVER PARTY

#3: MY TWO BEST FRIENDS

#4: LUCKY, LUCKY DAY

#5: THE GHOST IN MY CLOSET

#6: BALLET SURPRISE

#7: MAJOR LEAGUE TROUBLE

Based on the Hit TV Series!

Available from

A MINSTREL® BOOK

Published by Pocket Books